caillou

At the Amusement Park

Adaptation from the animated series: Marion Johnson
Illustrations: CINAR Animation and adapted by Éric Sévigny

 chouette ᒍINAP

Caillou has been riding in the car for a long, long time. When will they get to the amusement park?
"Are we there yet?" he asks Daddy.
"There yet?" Rosie repeats.
Daddy laughs. "Hold your horses. I think I see the amusement park up ahead."

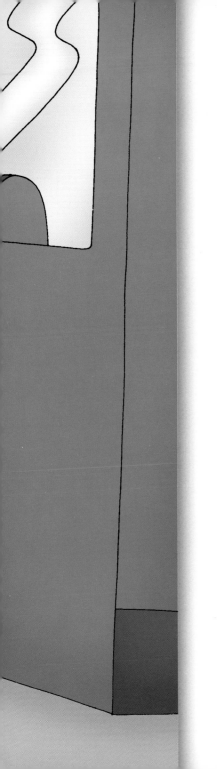

Caillou runs to get on the first ride.
"Stand next to the board, Caillou,"
says Daddy.
"Why?"
"You can't go on the River Ride if
you're too little," Daddy explains.
Caillou is just big enough!

Daddy and Caillou ride the
waves together.
"It's kind of scary, isn't it?" Daddy
says to Caillou.
"Yes," Caillou agrees. He's glad that
Daddy is also a little scared.
Soon Caillou is having too much fun
to be nervous. And so is Daddy.

"Here's the snack bar," says Daddy.
"Let's have lunch!"
Caillou and Rosie each get a hot dog.
What's for dessert? Daddy holds out
two big sticks of cotton candy.
"Cotton candy isn't really that good
for us," Mommy says.

The cotton candy melts in Caillou's mouth! Daddy has cotton candy for Mommy, too.

"Are you sure you don't want some?" he asks.

"It does look good," Mommy says, laughing and taking a taste.

"I guess it's okay once in a while."

After lunch, they take a ride on
the Ferris wheel.
The car rocks gently as it climbs all
the way to the top.
Caillou looks down.
"Mommy! Daddy! Look!" he shouts.
"You can see everything from up here!"

"There's the River Ride," says Daddy.
"And the merry-go-round,"
adds Mommy.
"And the snack bar," Caillou laughs.
Rosie giggles. "Yay!"

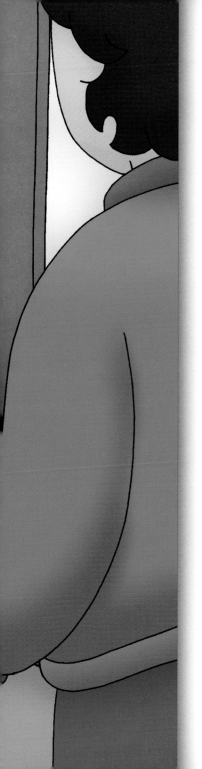

It's almost time to go home.
Suddenly Caillou sees something
really exciting—a huge teddy bear!
"Daddy, Daddy, look! Can we win
that prize?" he asks.
"Hmmm, you have to throw all three
hoops over that wooden block," says
Daddy. "Let's try!"

Caillou goes first.
All of his hoops fall on the ground.
The game is really hard.
Then Daddy takes his turn.
Caillou really, really wants
Daddy to win the big teddy bear.
One, two, three—all of Daddy's
hoops land on the block!

"What did you like the best,
Caillou?" asks Mommy on the way
home. "Was it the Ferris wheel?
Or the River Ride?"
Caillou shakes his head.
"I know," Mommy says. "It was the
teddy bear."
Caillou smiles. "The teddy bear is the
best of all!"

Text adapted by Marion Johnson from the scenario of the CAILLOU animated film series produced by CINAR Corporation (© 1997 Caillou Productions Inc., a subsidiary of CINAR Corporation). All rights reserved.
Original story written by Matthew Cope.
Illustrations taken from the television series CAILLOU and adapted by Éric Sévigny.
Graphic design: Marcel Depratto

Canadian Cataloguing in Publication Data

Johnson, Marion, 1949-
Caillou at the amusement park
(Scooter)
For children aged 3 and up.
Co-published by: CINAR Corporation.

ISBN 2-89450-380-6

1. Amusement parks - Juvenile literature. 2. Parent and child - Juvenile literature. I. CINAR Corporation. II. Title.

GV1851.J63 2003   j791'.06'8   C2002-941822-4

Legal deposit: 2003

We gratefully acknowledge the financial support of BPIDP and SODEC for our publishing activities.

Printed in Canada
10 9 8 7 6 5 4 3 2 1